OUTSIDE BROADCASTS

Dear Reader

My favourite sport to watch on television is tennis. I have often wondered how live tennis action is transmitted to TV screens so quickly! After investigating, I was so interested in the whole process of outside broadcasting, I decided to write about it.

> **YOU'LL MEET AN OUTSIDE-BROADCAST CAMERA OPERATOR WHO HAS FILMED SUBJECTS RANGING FROM SHARKS TO SHIPWRECKS TO DOG GAMES!**

Live broadcasts are filmed and transmitted by outside-broadcasting units, which are mini television studios inside large trucks.

In this book, I feature an outside-broadcasting company, The OB Group – it was interesting and fun observing the team at work. Join me behind the scenes to find out what happens during outside broadcasts – from camera to TV screen.

Enjoy!

Sharon Parsons

My sincere thanks to the following people for their time, information, images and enthusiasm for this book:

Colin Rothenberg, and the team at The OB Group, Sydney, Australia

Jamie Hurworth, Sydney, Australia

The Weather Channel, Sydney, Australia

Jason Speed, Melbourne, Australia

NELSON
CENGAGE Learning™
For learning solutions, visit **cengage.com.au**

Contents

OUTSIDE BROADCASTS

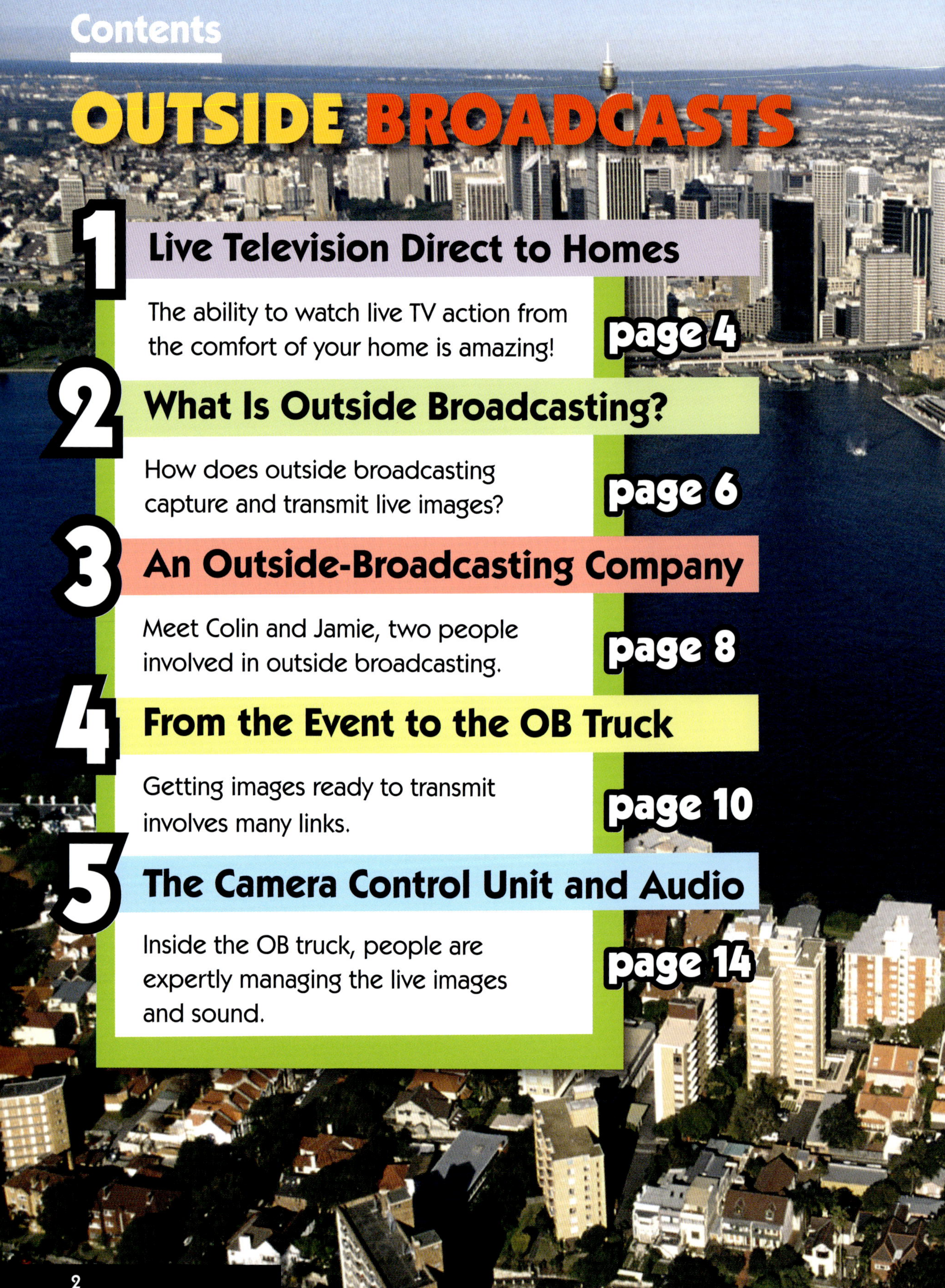

1 Live Television Direct to Homes

The ability to watch live TV action from the comfort of your home is amazing! page 4

2 What Is Outside Broadcasting?

How does outside broadcasting capture and transmit live images? page 6

3 An Outside-Broadcasting Company

Meet Colin and Jamie, two people involved in outside broadcasting. page 8

4 From the Event to the OB Truck

Getting images ready to transmit involves many links. page 10

5 The Camera Control Unit and Audio

Inside the OB truck, people are expertly managing the live images and sound. page 14

6 Directing What Viewers See at Home

As the action unfolds, the director is "calling the shots" so the viewer misses nothing.

page 16

7 Sports Replays

Missed a critical moment? A sports replay can show you exactly what happened.

page 18

8 A Television Floor Manager

Making sure everything, and everybody, is in the right place at the right time is vital.

page 20

9 Point, Zoom, Focus and Shoot!

The camera operators need to think and react fast to get the best shots.

page 24

10 The Best Job in the World – Outside-Broadcast Camera Operator

Could this just be the best job in the world?

TEXT TYPE
Exposition
PAGES 27–31

page 27

Index and Glossary page 32

1 Live Television Direct to Homes

Think about those times when you and your family have sat down excitedly in front of the television to watch a live broadcast of your favourite sporting event.

At the beginning of an event, reporters and presenters may appear on screen to provide commentary. Then, the vision may switch to glimpses of live action that may only last a few seconds, to set the scene before the full television coverage of the event begins.

"Goal!"

"How does it feel to have won the ice hockey championship again?"

Outside Broadcasting for Television

So who are the people behind the scenes deciding what vision you see? And what is the technology that enables you to see live vision of an event on your television screen? This form of broadcasting involves a team of technical people who work in remote locations from outside-broadcasting facilities.

a director edits footage in a television monitor room

a television monitor room at the Beijing Olympics (2010)

weather reporting on location

Social Studies

Live News and Weather Reports

Every day, television reporters present live reports so that viewers can get the most up-to-date news and weather. These reports can be presented from a location that is far away from the studio – even from another state or country. Presenters transmit their live coverage reports using outside-broadcasting facilities.

2 What Is Outside Broadcasting?

Outside broadcasting (OB) involves using a mobile unit with television production people to film and transmit events (news, sports and entertainment), via electronic and satellite technology to television studios (for broadcasting to people's homes). Below is one example of how live outside broadcasting works.

Live Outside Broadcasting

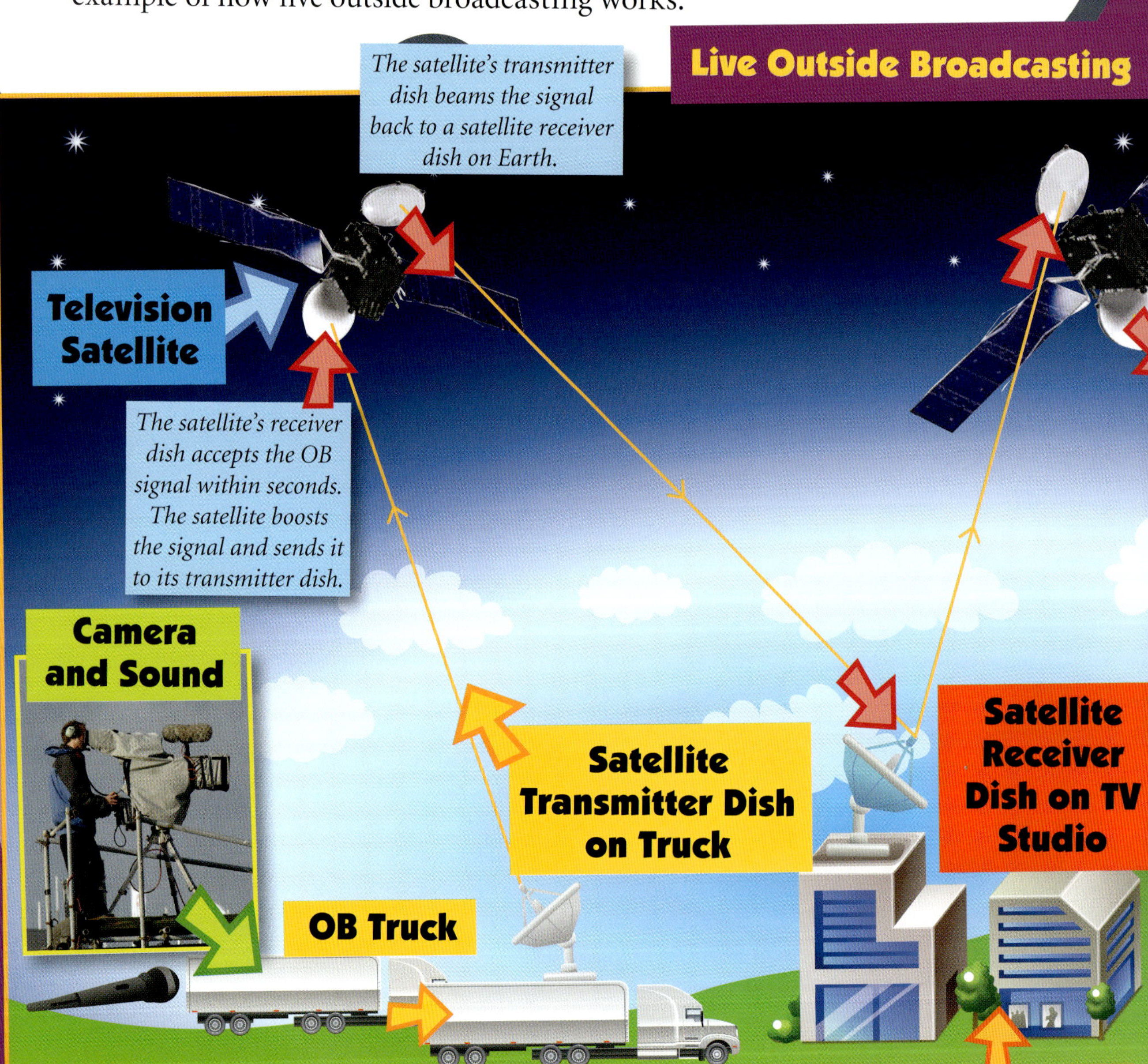

Outside-Broadcast Units

Outside-broadcast units are mobile, mini versions of television studios that are usually built inside a large truck or van. When an event that is being broadcast takes place over several days, an OB unit may be set up in a temporary on-site building.

The V8 Supercars events take place over several days, so the television team sets up their OB equipment in an on-site building.

Television Satellite

Viewers' Homes

Broadcasting Television Between Countries

DIRECT-TO-HOME BROADCASTING

"Direct-to-home" (DTH) broadcasting relates to the vision and sound that is transmitted via satellites to people's homes around the world.

An Outside-Broadcasting Company

The OB Group is an outside-broadcasting company based in Sydney, Australia. It works on behalf of television studios at public events, and broadcasts them live to viewers. Sometimes, they pre-record an event for the television studio.

Colin completes his technical checks before the live broadcasting begins.

Colin Rothenberg owns The OB Group, and his job at each event is to provide direction and technical support for his production team. His outside-broadcasting company specialises in televising outdoor news, sports and entertainment events, and they also film documentary programs.

Colin leaves the OB truck, satisfied that everything is ready for the live outside broadcast.

Colin's "Right-Hand Man"

Jamie is a camera operator who has worked with Colin for many years. He is multi-skilled in all areas of outside broadcasting, so he is often Colin's "right-hand man".

RIGHT-HAND MAN

"Right-hand man" is an old expression that is still used today to describe a trusted and helpful assistant.

Jamie Briefs a Camera Operator

Jamie Checks Each Camera's Vision

Jamie Films Event Vision

Jamie Checks the Video Monitors

4 From the Event to the OB Truck

The OB Group films and broadcasts events of all sizes. Depending on the event, they may require only one camera operator, or several.

An optical fibre system links vision from the camera on location, as well as the sound, to the outside broadcast truck.

1. Event

Key transmitting equipment in the field or on location

Video Transmitter

a camera operator focusing on attaining the best vision

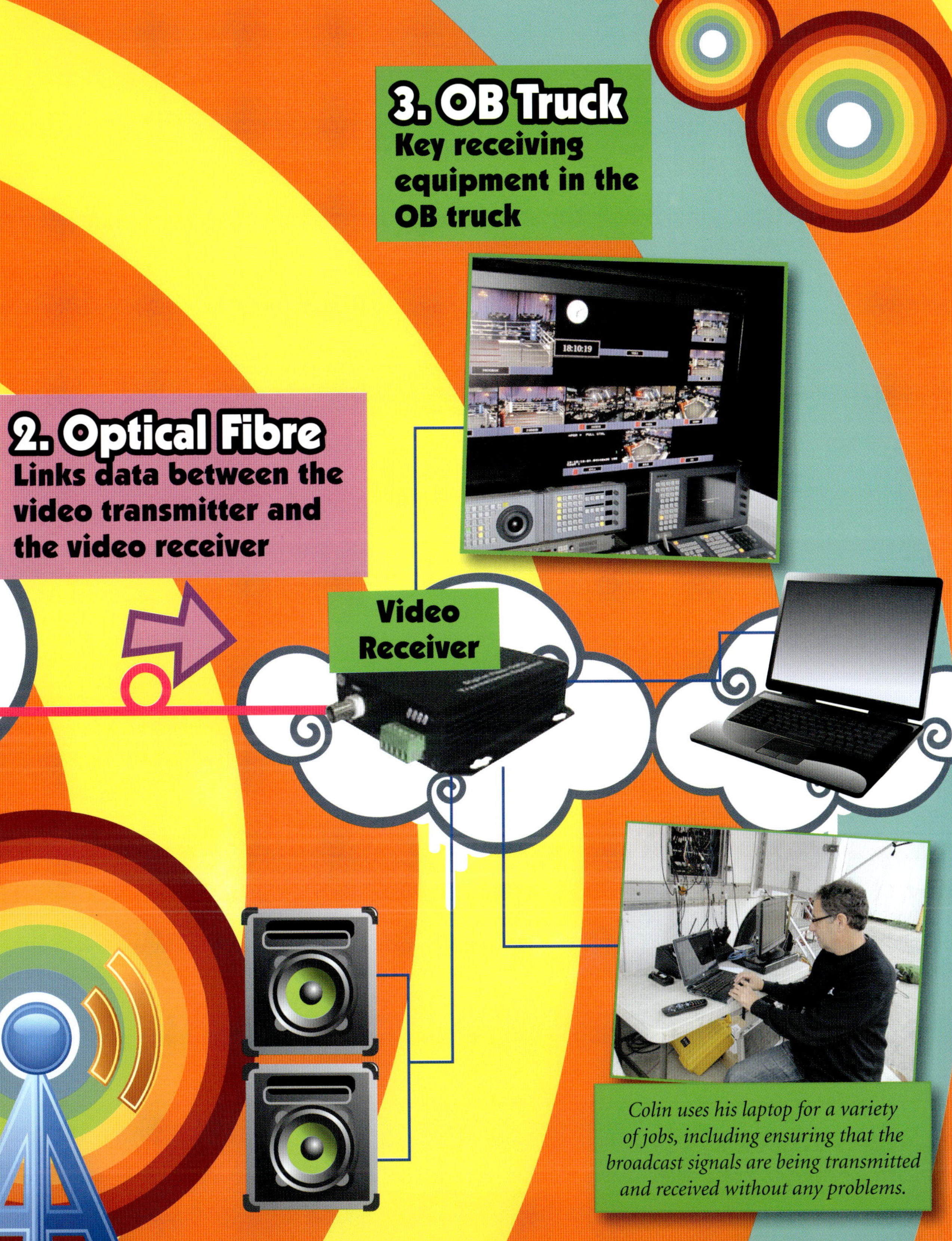

Colin uses his laptop for a variety of jobs, including ensuring that the broadcast signals are being transmitted and received without any problems.

Monitoring the Sound Levels
See page 15

LCD Video Monitor Wall

Directing the Best Vision for Home Viewers
See pages 16–17

Designing Graphics for the Screen
See page 16

Controlling the Cameras' Vision Quality
See page 14

Editing the Best Live Replays
See pages 18–19

The OB Truck Won't Fit!

When the OB truck can't be driven into a location, a smaller mobile broadcasting unit may be used. The equipment is easily packed into a crate and reassembled inside a small vehicle.

5 The Camera Control Unit and Audio

If you walk up the steps of The OB Group's main truck when it is set up for an event, you will see Dave busy at the camera control unit (CCU) and Chris working on audio. Their technical checks take several hours to complete before filming and broadcasting the event. Their attention to detail ensures that the camera vision and the audio controls are working perfectly.

WHAT'S A CCU?

A CCU (camera control unit) relates to the equipment that remotely controls some of the functions of the television cameras filming an event.

A CCU Operator

Dave is a CCU operator and his main role is to support the camera operators who are filming an event. While the camera operators concentrate on filming the best vision, the CCU operator can concentrate on technical matters, such as vision quality and colour consistency, for each camera.

Dave ensures that every camera's exposure looks the same so that viewers at home see the same colour tones when vision on TV switches between different cameras.

Audio Director

Chris is an audio director who works at a digital sound-mixing console to ensure that the sound waves are clearly transmitted from the sound operator's microphone (next to the camera operator) to the outside broadcast truck. At the sound-mixing console, Chris adjusts the levels of the sound so they are clear and consistent to the ear.

A Funny Story

Chris remembers a time when he "opened up" (turned on) a sound operator's microphone next to a toilet flushing, and viewers at home could hear the sounds!

Audio Assistant

An audio assistant works with the audio director and the camera operator. Their role involves dealing directly with the talent, either on set or at a sports event. One of their jobs is to get the right microphone to the right person at the right time, so that accurate and clear audio is ready for the audio director to put to air.

WHAT'S AUDIO?

Audio refers to the range of sound frequencies that the human ear can hear – from the lowest pitch to the highest pitch.

Chris at his sound-mixing console in the outside-broadcasting truck

Directing What Viewers See at Home

The LCD video monitor wall is at one end of The OB Group's truck, and the director's eyes quickly dart from screen to screen to decide which vision he or she wants viewers to see at home.

Every few seconds, the director will instruct the technical director to switch between video monitors so the event's action is sequential, as well as exciting and entertaining for viewers at home.

GRAPHICS OPERATOR

A graphics operator writes and designs the graphics and text to support the vision, including results, charts and graphs.

> EVERYONE WORKS FAST WHEN WE BROADCAST LIVE.
> COLIN

TECHNICAL DIRECTOR

A technical director is instructed by the director to switch between the video monitors, depending on what vision the director wants viewers to see at home.

DIRECTOR

A director needs to watch many video monitors and quickly decide on the best vision to broadcast to viewers.

7 Sports Replays

Viewers of sporting events like to see replays. The replay editors need to find the exact action footage to replay for viewers. This is a technically challenging job, as they need to work quickly, especially if it is a live broadcast. After a sporting event, the editors may need to find a selection of exciting action-replay footage for a post-event television broadcast and for the news. People also like to hear replays on the radio news, so an editor often needs to find some "sound grabs" that provide exciting audio for radio.

Lauryn enjoys the fast pace of live-replay editing.

Jack has to keep focused and work quickly to find the best replays for the director.

Pre-Recorded Events

Sometimes, an event is pre-recorded before it is broadcast on television. In these cases, Colin's technical director may "hand over" the footage to the television studio three hours before it is scheduled to be broadcast. So, in three hours, the television studio's production staff quickly review the footage. One of their jobs is to edit out over two hours of footage so that the event's highlights, plus commercials, will screen for one hour.

8 A Television Floor Manager

The floor manager is a senior role in television broadcasting because that person is in charge of all of the activity on the production floor. At outside-broadcasting facilities, the floor manager's role involves liaising with the team in the temporary studio at the event, and the team in the outside broadcast truck. The floor manager needs to do many jobs, including ensuring that all the equipment is in place, and making sure that all the technical checks have been done.

Floor manager Phil enjoys working at sporting events.

Qualities of a Good Floor Manager

- the ability to handle difficult situations calmly and diplomatically
- confidence and a strong work ethic
- excellent communication skills
- an understanding of the importance of being on time.

Live Event Liaison

The floor manager wears an earpiece and a microphone to maintain constant communication between the director (in The OB Group's truck) and the people on the floor (commentators, staff, talent and audience).

Phil checks that the commentators have everything that they need.

History

A Gaffer

A gaffer is an electrician. The term "gaffer" has its origins in pre-electricity times when motion picture studios relied on natural sunlight for their lighting. Large sheets of canvas were used to let in or block light. The sheets were moved around with hooks called "gaffs".

Lighting Technician

In television production, the lighting technician manages all the lights to ensure that the camera operators can film well-lit footage. Only a qualified electrician can work in the role of lighting technician.

HISTORY FEATURE

Australia's First Outside Broadcast

The first broadcasts to Australian viewers in their homes took place in September 1956. Television crews had two months to become familiar with the new technology before they broadcast the opening ceremony and other events of the Melbourne Olympic Games in November 1956.

ABC TV's outside-broadcasting van and staff

First OB Van

The Australian Broadcasting Corporation (ABC) had an OB van, which towed a trailer with a generator. When electrical power points were unavailable, the generator could provide the electricity to power the OB van. The OB van also travelled with a separate "links van", which provided a transmission link between the OB van and the television studio's tall transmitter on top of Gore Hill, Sydney, Australia. The ABC studios were on Gore Hill, too.

LITTLE TOOT

"Little Toot" was the ABC's name for its first temporary OB transmitter, which was used before the Gore Hill transmitter was built.

an original OB van used by the ABC

Ron Clarke lights the Olympic flame inside the cauldron at Melbourne's Olympic Games in 1956.

Olympic Games Events in Australia

Melbourne hosted Australia's first Olympic Games in 1956. It took 44 years for the Olympic Games to return to Australia, when it was held in Sydney in 2000.

	Melbourne 1956	Sydney 2000
Number of Nations Competing	72	199
Number of Sports	17	28
Number of Athletes	3 314	10 651

Melbourne 1956: 11% Women, 89% Men

Sydney 2000: 38% Women, 62% Men

A greater percentage of women competed in Sydney's Olympic Games than in Melbourne's Olympic Games.

First Olympic Games Competitor

Australia sent one competitor, Edwin Flack to the 1896 games. He became Australia's first gold medallist, winning the 800-metre and 1500-metre running races. He also competed in the marathon and tennis.

History

Australia and Greece

Australia and Greece are the only countries that have participated in every modern summer Olympic Games since they were first hosted in Athens, Greece in 1896.

Edwin Flack

9 Point, Zoom, Focus and Shoot!

Jamie is Colin's most experienced camera operator. He understands that he has to be ready to go anywhere at any time because television broadcasts happen 24 hours a day and seven days a week!

Jamie says that his work is like a circus because he is always travelling to new places, unpacking and setting up his camera gear, filming the scenes, repacking the gear and then travelling home. Jamie is asked to travel to many different places to film a diverse range of on-location events. He enjoys the variety of work and he gets a lot of personal satisfaction when he has done a great job.

Jamie films a bicycle race.

Jamie Films the World Dog Games

The World Dog Games is an event where dogs of all breeds and ages compete in fast-action events, such as flyball, dock-diving and agility. In 2009, Jamie was asked to film the first World Dog Games held in Sydney, Australia.

Joey is focused on getting to the ball as fast as possible.

Social Studies

Dog Sports

"Flyball" is a relay race run by teams of four dogs that take it in turns to complete various challenges.

"Dock-diving" is a competition in which dogs aim to jump the longest or highest distance into a pool of water.

"Agility" is a race where dogs compete on time and accuracy through an obstacle course.

Joey flies in the dock-diving competition!

Joey almost reaches her prize ball and ultimately wins the dock-diving competition at the World Dog Games in 2009!

Jamie at Jessica's Homecoming

In 2010, Jessica Watson became the youngest person to sail solo, non-stop and unassisted around the world.

At her homecoming to Sydney, Australia, in May 2010, Jamie was there to film Jessica's first steps onto the jetty to see her parents. Jamie recalls that Jessica's legs were wobbly as she stepped foot on land after seven months at sea.

As Jamie filmed 16-year-old Jessica Watson stepping from her yacht to the jetty, he captured the moment using different shots.

1. A **close-up shot** of Jessica on her boat.

2. A **zoomed out shot** shows more of Jessica's boat.

3. A **wide shot** shows the media surrounding Jessica with her parents on the jetty.

Health and Safety

Camera Assistant for Safety

Usually, a camera assistant will hold the cables for a camera operator and watch out for imminent dangers, such as steps.

10 The Best Job in the World – Outside-Broadcast Camera Operator

TEXT TYPE
Exposition
PAGES 27–31

Camera operators who work on outside broadcasts have the best job in the world! The best OB camera operators enjoy variety in their daily activities, travel the world and work in many challenging situations. While doing all this, they get to tell interesting stories via film. The job is definitely not run-of-the-mill. The following arguments support this claim.

Jamie prefers using a hand-held camera because he can move around more easily to capture the best shots.

Social Studies

What Makes a Good Camera Operator?

Jamie is a good camera operator because he is

- **able to work well in a team** *with many production staff members*
- **adaptable** *when it comes to working in many different places at different times of the day and night*
- **able to think quickly** *and film the most exciting footage for viewers*
- **strong and fit** *which helps him to carry a lot of equipment*
- **able to tell visual stories** *with a beginning, middle and an ending*
- **very experienced and qualified** *to film quality vision in many places.*

No Fear of Heights

First, OB camera operators do not typically work in nine-to-five jobs. In fact, they often work in many different settings and conditions. For example, to get footage of people taking part in extreme or action sports, such as abseiling or parachuting, a camera operator may fly in a helicopter near the competitors to capture a real sense of the excitement involved. Sometimes, to get the "action" shots and close-ups, the camera operator may even participate. In such instances, it is useful not to have a fear of heights!

Jamie is ready for lift off

Jamie Has No Fear of Heights

Jamie is a trained abseiler, which means he can film rock climbers. He recalls a time when his fearlessness helped him to film kite flying from the inside of a helicopter. In 2010, a group of Japanese kite flyers wanted to break the world altitude record for kite flying in Kings Canyon, Northern Territory, Australia. Jamie had to film the kites darting quickly in many directions. The helicopter door was removed but, to keep Jamie safe, he was harnessed to the chopper. Despite the mighty wind gusts whipping his face, he managed to film from the floor and the skids of the helicopter.

That day, the world record was not broken – the record-holder is still Canadian kite flyer, Richard Synergy, who flew his single kite at 4422.3 metres (14 509 feet).

kite-flying

KINGS CANYON

Kings Canyon is in the Watarrka National Park in the Northern Territory, Australia. It is a four-hour drive west from Uluru. The red rock face of the canyon rises over 100 metres above the forests to provide shelter from the harsh surrounding desert. Visitors can do many walks that include the tropical pools in the Garden of Eden and the beehive rock formations called the Lost City.

No Fear of Filming Underwater

Second, OB camera operators often work in interesting surroundings. Sometimes, this may involve filming underwater for documentaries and reports. For example, some jobs may include diving in underwater caves, around shipwrecks and with marine animals. Opportunities like these make the job of a camera operator very thrilling!

Jamie Enjoys Filming Underwater

Jamie has been diving since he was a teenager and his diving qualification comes in handy when he films underwater documentaries.

In 1988, his first job involved filming in underwater caves beneath the Nullarbor Desert in South Australia, Australia.

"THE CAVES WERE DARK AND FELT DANGEROUS."
JAMIE

the entrance to the Nullarbor caves

NULLARBOR'S UNDERWATER CAVES

About 90 metres below the red dust of the Nullarbor Desert lie some of the world's largest underground cave systems. The dark, cold cave tunnels spread out for many kilometres and they lead down to subterranean lakes and rivers.

Jamie Films Sharks

Imagine Jamie with his back pressed up against a rock face deep underwater – but to complicate the situation, he is facing 50 hammerhead sharks!

Jamie's job was to film a shark-feeding frenzy and that's exactly what he did. His camera rolled as the fish bait sank down from the boat above, and he filmed the swift action of 50 sharks quickly swimming about as they competed for every fish.

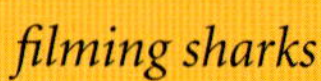

filming sharks

Jamie Films Shipwrecks

When diving around shipwrecks, a camera operator must not disturb the historic remains. This includes not touching or entering the shipwreck and not removing any relics. This is important for preserving the historic significance of a site and showing respect for the past.

Jamie has dived to depths up to 100 metres around the Great Barrier Reef in Queensland, Australia, to film shipwrecks for documentaries.

filming a shipwreck

Social Studies

Filming Ocean Animals

When diving with animals, it is important to respect the animals and their environment. This is essential not only for the safety of the animals, but it can also make a big difference to the quality of a camera operator's footage. The best animal documentaries include footage of animals undisturbed in their natural environment.

GREAT BARRIER REEF SHIPWRECKS

There are about 1 600 known shipwrecks at the bottom of Marine Park at Queensland's Great Barrier Reef.

The shipwrecks have become home to thousands of marine animals so it is important that the area is protected from human interference.

Tell a Story

Finally, OB camera operators get to combine their technical and creative skills to make imaginative and visually interesting stories for others to enjoy. The best scenes – no matter how long – include a beginning, middle and an ending. To do this, OB camera operators work out how best to sequence their shots so that the scenes tell the story smoothly and logically. To keep a story flowing, an OB camera operator needs to think quickly because there's no time to talk about an idea with anyone else. In fact, the requirement to think on their feet to get the best footage is perhaps the most challenging, but also the most rewarding, part of the job for OB camera operators.

The Best Job

Although an OB camera operator's job may be demanding, it is far from boring. They work in many different places around the world and experience a variety of situations. In addition, the challenge to excite viewers with a unique vision means that OB camera operators definitely have the most interesting job of them all!

Film and View the Action in Sequence

The illustrations below give an example of a four-shot camera sequence when filming a go-kart race.

1

Camera 1: viewers see the front of the red go-kart racing up to a sharp corner.

2

Camera 2: a close-up shot of the red go-kart from behind as it leaves the sharp corner.

3

Camera 3: a zoomed-out shot follows the red go-kart along a straight part of the track.

4

Camera 3 second shot: a wide-angle shot of the red go-kart as it overtakes the others.

Index

camera control unit 14

camera operator 9, 10, 14, 15, 21, 24, 26, 27–31

digital 15

earpiece 21

editor 18

floor manager 20–21

gaffer 21

graphics 16

microphone 15, 21

replay 18

reporter 4, 5

sound grab 18

sound wave 15

vision 4, 5, 7, 10, 14, 16, 17, 27, 31

Glossary

director	The person who is in charge of deciding how a television program is made
monitor	A screen that shows what a camera is filming
optical fibre system	A series of cables that can link outdoor television cameras back to the equipment in a studio or a truck
pre-record	To record a television program before it is broadcast
presenter	A person who appears on a television program, talking to the camera
satellite	A spacecraft that sends and receives television signals
studio	A room in which television programs are filmed
talent	People who appear on a television program
viewer	A person who watches a television program